THE TECHNOLOGY OF THE ANCIENT WORLD™

THE TECHNOLOGY OF ANCIENT JAPAN

Meg Greene

The Rosen Publishing Group, Inc., New York

For my special friend Max Henrie

Published in 2006 by The Rosen Publishing Group, Inc.
29 East 21st Street, New York, NY 10010

Library of Congress Cataloging-in-Publication Data

Greene, Meg.
The technology of ancient Japan / Meg Greene.—1st ed.
    p. cm.—(The technology of the ancient world)
Includes bibliographical references and index.
ISBN 1-4042-0559-4 (library binding: alk. paper)
1. Technology—Japan—History—To 1500—Juvenile literature. 2. Japan—Civilization—
To 794—Juvenile literature.
I. Title. II. Series.

T27.J3G74 2005
609.52—dc22

2005014487

Manufactured in the United States of America

On the cover: A black lacquer writing box from the seventeenth century (the Edo period in Japan) inlaid with copper foil, gold, and mother-of-pearl is superimposed on a circa 1800 Japanese woodcut showing a man doing carpentry in the Totomi Mountains. The woodcut, called *In the Totomi Mountains*, is by Hokusai.

CONTENTS

ANCIENT JAPANESE TECHNOLOGY: SOMETHING BORROWED

The first people to discover Japan arrived there almost 35,000 years ago. Many of these early settlers came from northern China, southern Russia, and the Korean Peninsula. These migrations marked the beginning of a culture that continues to fascinate and charm the world. Modern Japan is among the world's economic superpowers and is a leader in technological innovation and development. Many advancements in travel, communications, and entertainment—cars, cell phones, televisions, and video games, for example—have come from Japanese designers, engineers, and scientists.

From approximately 10,000 BC to AD 1185, the Japanese borrowed, adapted, and often improved upon technology from other cultures, particularly those of China and Korea. The result is a rich and multifaceted culture whose technological developments are celebrated for being distinctly Japanese in their creativity, design, and usage.

This woodblock for a newspaper (from 1924) is an example of one of the wonderful technological advances that was enhanced by the ancient Japanese. Especially known for their masterful skill at depicting scenes of daily life, as well as magical evocations of the beautiful Japanese landscape, woodcuts are an ancient art form that the Japanese excelled at.

THE TECHNOLOGY OF LIFE

Japanese technology used to gather and produce food dates back more than 10,000 years. Over time, Japan slowly changed from a society of hunter-gatherers to a people who adapted to their natural resources in order to nourish themselves. In bringing about this transformation, the Japanese altered the way they obtained food from the land and the sea. To understand and explain such a transition, archaeologists have concentrated on learning how the Japanese used technology to hunt, fish, and farm.

Fruit of the Sea

The earliest Japanese technology associated with the acquisition of food has been traced to the Jomon period, which dates from approximately 10,000 to 1000 BC. The people of the Jomon era were

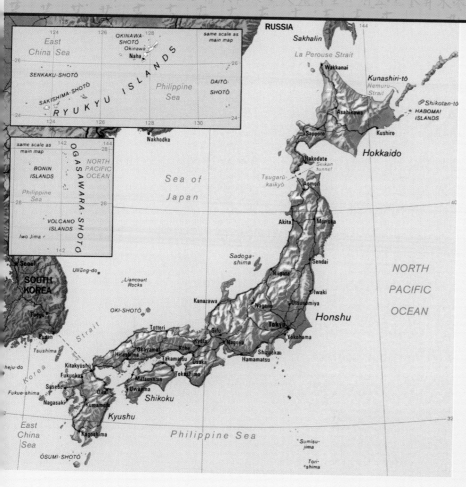

This map of Japan shows the four main islands that make up the country. They are Hokkaido, Honshu, Shikoku, and Kyushu. These islands stretch approximately 1,500 miles (2,400 kilometers) from the northeast to the southwest. The majority of the major cities in Japan—including Tokyo (which was called Edo in ancient times)—are situated on Honshu.

migratory—they traveled from place to place in search of food. Depending on the time of the year, their diet consisted of nuts, various plants and tubers that grew wild, meat, and different kinds of fish and shellfish.

Archaeologists have discovered fishing equipment in northern Japan. Antler harpoons and wooden dugout canoes suggest that the ancient Japanese relied on fishing to supplement their diet. While their technology was very basic, it appears to have been

effective. Archaeologists speculate that Japanese fishermen hunted dolphins and tuna with harpoons. Smaller fish, including sardines and mackerel, swam in the bays and inlets along the coast. These were caught with nets made of vines, rope, and small stone and clay weights.

The Jomon people also constructed fishing weirs, or walls. Made of woven sticks such as willow or oak, the weir operated as a series of small fences that guided fish into

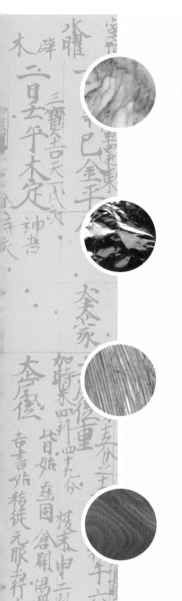

ANCIENT ANGLERS

The discovery of bone and antler fish hooks and pumice floats suggests that the Japanese engaged in angling. Angling is when a fisherman uses a hook, line, and rod or pole to catch fish. These early poles were usually made from bamboo. They measured between twelve and fifteen feet (approximately three and half to four and a half meters) in length. The first fishing lines were probably made from animal hair; later they were made of silk. By the seventh century AD, many Japanese nobles preferred to fish for sport.

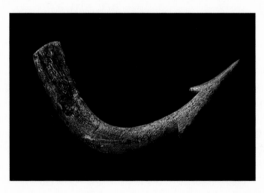

This barbed fishhook was skillfully carved from a deer antler, a material Japanese artisans have worked with since Paleolithic times. It dates from the Jomon period.

enclosed spaces. This way, they were caught easily.

The Hunt

The people of the Jomon period hunted wild boars, deer, rabbit, frogs, squirrels, and wolves. Simple stone or flint arrowheads and spear points found by archaeologists suggest that the Jomon people knew how to make and use such weapons. They also dug oval pits in which wild game were trapped. When animals fell or were chased into the pits, they were easier to kill. One type of pit was made from a series of poles that suspended a captured animal above the ground.

Fruit of the Earth

The Jomon people also relied on gathering plants, fruit, and nuts. They used chipped stone axes fashioned from slate or flint. Although it is called an axe, archaeologists believe this tool was not used to chop wood but to dig wild yams and other tubers from the ground.

Tending the Land

By 1000 BC, the Yayoi culture (300 BC to AD 300) replaced the Jomon culture, introducing more sophisticated technologies of food production. Among the most important innovations was the development of bronze and iron tools. Historians believe that immigrants from China and Korea brought this new technology to Japan.

Now a staple of the Japanese diet, rice came to Japan comparatively late. With the introduction of wet-paddy rice farming around 300 BC, the Japanese established more stable farming communities. In turn, the

cultivation of rice facilitated population growth and the emergence of a more sophisticated division of labor, with workers performing more specialized tasks.

An indication that, at first, the Yayoi people grew only dry rice was

Wet-rice farming was an important part of ancient Japanese culture. This man is plowing a rice paddy with help from his ox. As the traditional Japanese diet was based on rice, this was a very important industry. At present, rice cultivation is declining as modern Japanese eat more pasta and bread.

NUTS!

The discovery of pits as large as 7 feet (approximately 2 m) deep and 7 feet in diameter provide more insight into the Jomon diet. Many varieties of nuts, including chestnuts, horse chestnuts, walnuts, and acorns were found in the pits. To make the nuts edible, the Jomon people softened them by soaking or boiling. The presence of grinding stones and stone mortars further suggests that they also ground nuts into flour to make biscuits that were then stored in beautiful earthenware pots.

the construction of settlements on hills or high ground instead of in low-lying, marshy areas near rivers or along the coast. Those were ideal for wet-paddy rice farming.

Chinese and Korean immigrants introduced wet-paddy rice cultivation to Japan. Fashioning primitive plows from wood and metal, they excavated and flooded small plots for planting, adding and removing water according to a schedule. Weeding was an ongoing process done to ensure that paddies produced the maximum yield.

In adapting this method of rice farming, the Japanese first marked the outlines of the paddy with wooden stakes. They then dug irrigation canals to channel water to the fields and constructed drains to remove it. In addition, they built structures in which to store the crop. They even adopted (from the Chinese) a special heavy wooden shoe, the *tianxiautuo*, worn by rice farmers working in the paddies.

Life's Tools

With the introduction of iron around 500 BC, the Japanese began to make a number of different tools based on Chinese designs. These included an axe, a crescent-shaped harvesting knife, and stronger, more durable plows and hoes. In addition to

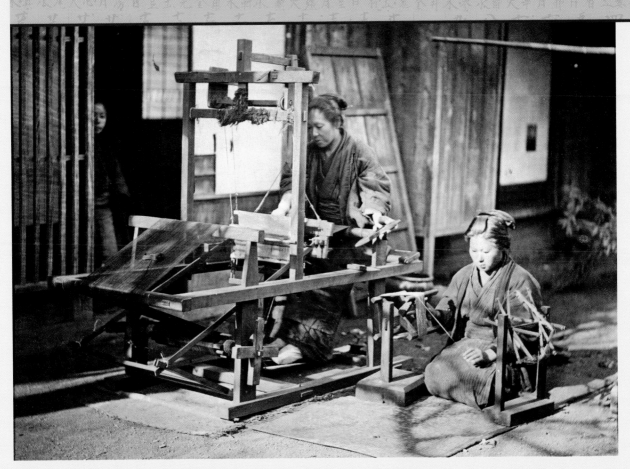

The textile trade was very important in ancient Japan. Weaving looms and spinning wheels were painstakingly built so that they would be durable. There were mainly four kinds of fibers used in Japanese textiles: hemp, ramie, cotton, and silk.

new tools, Yayoi potters—usually women—created a wide range of cooking, storage, and serving vessels.

Clothing a People

By the late third century AD, Koreans introduced sewing, and later, weaving techniques to Japan. With these two new technologies, the ancient Japanese developed what became a vibrant textile industry that included a spectacular range of woven and dyed fabrics.

The Japanese manufacture of textiles began with the weaving of simple twisted cords made from wisteria and mulberry fibers with hemp and ramie grass. A gift of silk clothes and silkworms from the Chinese court to Japanese royalty spurred the development of Japanese silk. From the fourth century, the Japanese court enthusiastically supported textile and silk production, encouraging weavers from China and Korea to exhibit their latest fabrics.

Among the many new innovations the Koreans and Chinese introduced was the technique for making colorful brocades and delicate silk gauzes. By the eighth century, during the Nara period (AD 710 to 794), the Japanese began using a variety of stamp-applied, wax-resistant dyed fabrics and embroidery techniques, which had also originated in China. A native Japanese method of working with textiles, which emerged during the eighth century, was Kyo Yuzen, a traditional dyeing technique that used hand-drawn patterns. By the beginning of the Heian period in the late eighth century (794 to 1185), the Japanese had refined their artistic style, favoring plain silks over woven and dyed designs.

THE TECHNOLOGY OF EXPRESSION

The Japanese excelled in the visual and literary arts. With few exceptions, the Japanese borrowed many of these techniques from China. As with other cultural transfers, they adapted the new forms to fit their own needs. In the process, they created some of the most distinctive aspects of Japanese culture.

The Tools of Writing

Before the fourth century AD, when the Kofun period (300 to 710) began, the Japanese had no system of writing. However, increased contact with China led the Japanese to adapt Chinese script. From this already ancient technique, the Japanese created a unique language. They also developed printing and calligraphy, thus creating a stunning and distinct visual language.

The characters numbered 1 and 3 are kanji, and those numbered 2 and 4 are hiragana. Kanji charaters stand for objects, while Hiragana characters stand for syllables. Character 2 is pronounced as "oh" while character 4 is pronounced as "ah." Character 1 is similar in meaning to the English prepositions "on" or "at." Character 3 means something similar to the word "peace."

Alphabet

The adoption of Chinese written characters—kanji—occurred gradually, beginning at the end of the fourth century AD. By the seventh century, during the Heian period (794 to 1185), many Japanese scholars, especially Buddhist monks, had traveled to China. This further popularized kanji writing.

The earliest Chinese characters pictured the represented object. In time, the Japanese modified this system to write words borrowed from Chinese or native Japanese words that had similar meanings. However, the Japanese continued to use Chinese phonetics to develop elements of grammar.

In the seventh and eighth centuries, the Japanese invented another writing technique based on Chinese characters called kana, which means "borrowed words." The most important innovation in Japanese writing occurred with the introduction of hiragana, in which each character represents a single syllable. Not only is hiragana easier and faster to write, it also does not require knowledge of Chinese characters.

This five-volume book of woodblock prints dating from 1797 illustrates the ancient process of papermaking in Japan. In later periods, aside from simply being a surface for writing, more uses for Japanese paper were developed. For example, screens and sliding doors were also crafted out of paper.

Paper

Paper first appeared in Japan around the sixth century. The Japanese learned the process of papermaking from a Korean Buddhist monk named Don-cho. To make paper pulp, the Japanese used the fibers of hemp, rattan, mulberry, bamboo, rice, straw, and seaweed. The pulp was then rolled out and dried. The Japanese did the majority of their writing on scrolls called *kansubon*. These became the most common book form in Japan until the tenth century.

In ancient Japan, intricate, beautiful, and highly decorative patterns and symbols were carved into the surface of wooden blocks like this one. As traditional Japanese writing was vertical rather than horizontal, the columns of this woodblock would be read from top to bottom. Similar blocks were used to design textiles.

To write on their paper, the Japanese used another invention borrowed from the Chinese: india ink. Originally designed for blackening the surfaces of raised stone-carved hieroglyphics, ink was created out of a mixture of soot from burnt pine, lamp oil, and musk. The Japanese improved upon this recipe by experimenting with natural dyes and colors that came from berries, plants, and minerals. In early writings, they used different colored inks, with a ritual meaning attached to each color. Using sticks and simple brushes, the writer carefully applied ink to paper, and later to wooden blocks made for printing.

Printing

The Japanese use of ink also had an important influence on a form of block printing they had developed around the eighth century. Earlier, the Chinese had developed the process of block printing, but the Japanese innovation, although quite simple, produced more elegant results. Requiring no machinery, Japanese printers instead relied on a few tools for cutting designs into planks of cherry wood. Then, they applied ink to the block and rubbed a round, flat pad over it to imprint the design on paper. The inks used were simple, consisting of a mixture of water and paste made from rice flour. Artists in Japan still use this style of printing.

THE ART OF PAPER

Besides learning how to make paper, the Japanese also practiced the art of paper-folding that originated in China. Origami, the technique of delicately folding papers into an astonishing array of designs and shapes, had a tremendous impact on Japanese art, culture, life, and thought.

This origami crane is one of the more traditional figures that is part of the rich tradition of shapes that are made in Japanese paper folding. The crane is symbolic of health, happiness, and peace. Even in the cases of extremely complex designs, nothing other than a piece of paper is used.

Calligraphy

Buddhist monks introduced calligraphy to Japan sometime during the seventh century. Calligraphic script, which is highly artful, was written using special bamboo brushes that were made by skilled artisans. The bristles for the tip came from animals such as wolves, squirrels, weasels, and badgers. The calligrapher made short, firm stokes with the pen to produce stylized characters. Unlike the pens that the Chinese often used when doing calligraphy, the Japanese brushes allowed for greater control over the thickness and quality of the characters, thus producing a far more elegant script.

Sumi-e

The Japanese also developed the art of *sumi-e*, or ink-stick painting. Sumi-e first emerged in China, but by the ninth century, the Japanese began using it. The style is known for relying on one color (almost always black) to create an image. The ink was made by mixing the soot of burning pine twigs with resin. The ink stick was made with the help of a *suzuri*, or ink stone, which was used to grind down the stick.

Ceramics

The visual arts in Japan began more than 12,000 years ago. Based on the remains of early pottery, archaeologists and art historians believe that the Jomon culture developed ceramics long before any other culture. Of even greater interest, the pottery dates to before agriculture took hold in Japan. The pottery that the Jomon created was not only functional, it was of exceptionally high quality.

Jomon pottery probably started with several coils or loops of clay on a flat surface. When potters finished a piece, they placed it in an open pit and fired it at low heat. When dried, the stacked coils and the raised lines gave the pottery a "roped" look—hence the name Jomon or "roped." To make other designs, Jomon potters used their fingers or string. By 2500 BC, they began producing decorated humanlike figurines known as *dogu*.

The Yayoi also produced pottery, but of an even more sophisticated nature. Yayoi pottery was noted for geometric shapes and decoration.

Dotaku (ritual bells) from the Yayoi period were thought to have originated in China, where they were used as cattle bells. As the ancient Japanese did not engage in cattle farming, these bells were probably present in Japanese rituals for their symbolism as opposed to being practical objects. A further reason for this belief is that the sound produced by the bells was extremely muffled.

These potters worked on wheels and fired the clay at hotter temperatures. The Yayoi also used bronze technology that arrived from Korea. With this knowledge, they created bell-shaped pieces known as *dotaku*.

Lacquer

The Japanese are renowned for their beautiful lacquerware. Lacquer is a waterproof varnish made by layering numerous coats of sap taken from a lacquer tree. Although the tree originated in China, the Japanese developed lacquering techniques between 5,000 and 6,000 years ago. They used lacquer as an adhesive to attach arrowheads to arrows. Almost a thousand years later, they developed a way to tint the lacquer in red and black and use it to coat tableware, daily utensils, weapons, and accessories such as combs and earrings. Around AD 400, a guild specializing in the lacquer arts, called Urushi-be, was established.

Making lacquer was a long, difficult process. First, lacquer juice was collected from the tree and filtered to remove impurities. Then the lacquer was colored using pigment or oil to produce a tinted, glossy liquid. The

This type of red-lacquered helmet (known as a *kabuto* in Japanese), which dates from nineteenth-century Japan, was known for being easy to make. Along with the crest-holders at the front and back of the helmet, the neck guard would have served to protect a warrior's neck from being penetrated by sword or spear points.

lacquer was then applied and left to dry. This process was repeated several times. The result was a beautifully coated object of deep color and rich shine.

Painting

By the late eighth century, Japanese art had evolved into something truly distinctive. With the creation of new techniques for painting, the Japanese produced beautiful artworks that recorded all aspects of life.

An exciting new painting style developed. Known as *emakimono*, or illustrated manuscripts, the scrolls incorporated scenes painted in many colors or simple black ink drawings. To create the scrolls, the artist joined several dozen sheets of paper or, occasionally, silk. A cover was attached to one end and a roller to the other.

A typical emakimono measured 1 foot (30 centimeters) in width and 30 to 40 feet (9 to 12 m) in length. The scrolls were read horizontally and handled carefully to keep the delicate paper from tearing.

Japanese painters also began adding their signatures, with name seals known as *hanko*, to their works. Cut by hand into jade (for the emperor and nobility) or copper (for the general public), these engraved stamps were an indication of a painting's authenticity. The hanko were dipped in pigment (usually red).

Artists used several plants and minerals to make their paints. Malachite and azurite (a rare blue stone), for example, combined to produce cobalt green. A mixture of calcium carbonate, calcium phosphate, and selected oyster shells produced white. Other materials included tigereye and quartz. Japanese artists also made use of volcanic glass. When crystallized, the glass was mixed with paint to make it more vivid.

THE BUILDING ARTS

A distinct Japanese architecture emerged as early as the Yayoi period. With the introduction of Buddhism to Japan during the sixth century, the influence of Chinese and Korean styles began to overshadow native Japanese construction. Nonetheless, even the popularity of foreign styles could not diminish the Japanese preference for using natural materials and integrating exterior and interior space. The result was an architectural style that has enjoyed worldwide popularity.

Early Dwellings

The majority of structures built before the Yayoi period were very basic. For instance, Jomon pit houses usually consisted of several wooden perimeter posts surrounding a round or rectangular pit that measured between 2 and 2.5 feet (30–40 cm) deep. The posts generally leaned in toward the center or formed an A-frame. These

This is a reconstruction of a late Jomon-period home in the town of Kizukuri in Aomori Prefecture. Aomori is located at the northern-most point of the main island of Honshu. It faces the island of Hokkaido. Considering that the Jomon culture is called "tree culture," it is not surprising that trees and wood were essential to the construction of daily utensils and dwellings such as the one above.

were joined together with vines or rope. The entire structure was covered with thatch, except for the doorway and a hole in the roof that allowed smoke to escape. For heating, these homes usually had a fireplace made of stone or earthenware.

Although more settled agricultural communities began to appear during the Yayoi period, the Japanese continued to design their homes according to the pattern established during the Jomon era. The dwellings of the early Yayoi period were square-shaped and topped by thatched roofs that reached to the ground. In the center of a home's earthen floor was a hearth.

The Yayoi people also built structures such as wood rice storehouses with raised floors that were similar in style to those already found in China. These storehouses had a profound impact on Japanese architecture, and

A SIMPLE MOUND?

A kofun mound was more than a pile of dirt. On the exterior was the *tukuridashi*, a protruding platform connected to a narrow part of the mound. A *shugou* or moat, was dug to protect the kofun from brigands. Its shape was either similar to a keyhole or a horse's hoof. Inside the mound was the coffin, which was made of wood, stone, or earthenware and usually shaped like a house, a roof, or a boat. A pit- or cave-styled stone chamber protected the coffin. Pit-styled chambers were completely enclosed by ceiling stones. Cave-styled chambers had a stone door and a passage leading to the outside.

are, in fact, considered to be the models for modern Shinto shrines.

The Great Mounds

During the Kofun period, the Japanese built tombs, known as *kofun*, from large earthen mounds. The practice of constructing burial mounds began during the Yayoi period when both round and square mounds with moats were the norm.

In AD 300, the Japanese made even greater innovations by building keyhole-shaped mounds, known as *zempô-kôen-fun*. Although most circular and square mounds were small, measuring less than 165 feet (50 m) in diameter, the keyhole-shaped mounds sometimes exceeded 1,300 feet (400 m). Given the size of the keyhole mounds, archaeologists and historians believe that they were the burial sites of royalty or other important figures.

Building the mounds required huge amounts of time and labor. In 1995, one of Japan's leading civil engineering firms copied the process. Engineers estimated that workers would have had to remove 26.1 million cubic feet (740,000 cubic meters) of soil and 14,000 tons of stone. The entire process would likely have taken fifteen years to complete and have consumed 7 million man-days of

This beautiful example of an ancient Japanese five-story pagoda was part of the temple called Horyuji in Nara. The temple was built by Crown Prince Shotoku according to the wishes of Emperor Yomei, and was dedicated to Buddha. A great fire in AD 670 destroyed the original pagoda.

labor. In today's currency, the cost of building the largest mounds would have amounted to more than $800 million. Clearly, construction of the kofun mounds remains one of the greatest feats in the history of architecture.

Architecture of Wood

Because the Japanese islands are volcanic and stone was not plentiful, wood became the preferred building material by the fifth century. Japanese architecture became more intricate. During this period, unlike the structures of the Chinese (which were covered with paint) the Japanese emphasized the natural beauty of the materials used.

Another radical departure from Chinese architecture was the granary, which had been in use since the early Yayoi period. Granaries were elevated wood structures designed to house rice. They were built on a scaffold, with steep steps made of wood or stone. These steps lead to the entrance.

The Japanese also developed other imaginative building technologies. For instance, they devised one of the earliest forms of air-conditioning for the Shosoin storehouse near the temple called Todaiji in Nara. Built in the middle of the eighth century, the storehouse was constructed to preserve the temple's many treasures from the heat and humidity of Japanese summers.

The secret to Japanese air-conditioning was in its method of construction, known as *azekurazukuri*. Walls were made from horizontally stacked *azeki*, or cross-sections of lumber. Each cross-section was triangular, allowing water to drain efficiently and preventing damp air from lingering in the storehouse.

By nature, wood expands as it absorbs moisture. As the azeki slowly dried out, the wood shrunk and small spaces in the walls opened, which promoted ventilation. This natural method of air-conditioning has kept the inside of the Shosoin storehouse dry and preserved the treasures within for centuries. Without this inventive technology, rare and valuable cultural artifacts might have been damaged or destroyed.

Another technique that Japanese builders used was the "pileup" structure. For example, when building a five-story pagoda, workers assembled the framework for each layer. They then raised, or "piled up," each layer—one above another—like stacked pen caps.

Each layer was then connected to the next. In this way, the Japanese could construct much taller buildings, many of which are considered architectural masterpieces.

The Nightingale Floor

A fascinating development in Japanese architecture was the invention of singing floors. These so-called nightingale floors were deliberately warped and had holes strategically cut into them. When someone walked across such a floor, the pressure of the person's weight pushed the floorboards against rubber clamps used to hold them in place. This would force air through the holes and produce various tonalities. To the Japanese, the sound the floor made was so beautiful that they likened it to the song of the nightingale.

The Growth of an Industry

As the construction of new buildings in Japan increased, so did technological advancements. Meanwhile, more artisans arrived from China and Korea. They brought with them knowledge of iron technology. Soon, a professional guild, or organization, of metal artisans was established.

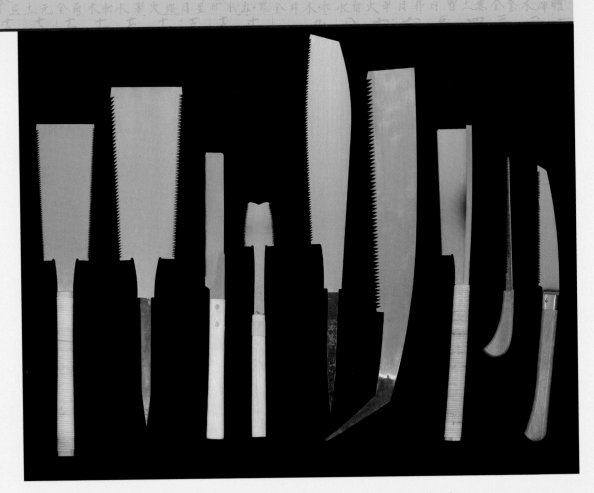

This wonderful array of ancient carpentry tools includes various types of planes, hammers, adzes, saws, and chisels. In particular, ancient Japanese carpentry is known for its distinctive use of elaborate joints. Using some of the tools featured here, wooden structures were built without the use of nails or glue.

Members of the guild produced a great variety of iron tools. Archaeological evidence dating from between the fourth and sixth centuries uncovered a wide and amazing array of tools used for building. Many of these are still in use today. They included flat and iron-handled axes, adzes, flat and circular chisels, square and spiral gimlets, and hammers. Another important discovery was that many of the tools were standardized, meaning that they had the same shape, blade width, and handle type.

To prepare the wood for building, carpenters shaved it with a chisel to smooth the timber and remove imperfections. Using a saw or axe, they then cut the timber in half and marked the spots in ink where they would make additional cuts.

To position the large supports of a building, the Japanese relied on the windlass, a simple crane system. First, the timber to be put in place was marked; workers then tied ropes around the marked areas and attached them to a smaller windlass, which was connected to a large windlass that was supported by a tower. By pulling the ropes, workers guided the support into place.

One other building innovation that the Japanese used were kites, especially when at work on tall structures. Baskets attached to kites were filled with needed supplies. Workers on the ground flew the kites to workers on the building. This ingenious technique allowed construction to proceed at a faster pace.

THE ART OF WAR

By the early second century AD, the Japanese believed that the development of military technology was just as vital as the development of agriculture or architecture. To make weaponry and armor, the Japanese once again blended superior workmanship with decorative elements to produce weapons that were as lethal was they were beautiful.

Armor

The earliest pieces of armor found in Japan date from the second century AD. Based on statues found at burial sites, it appears that early armor—made of large iron plates attached by leather thongs—was used by foot soldiers. To cover the legs and upper arms, soldiers wore iron plates tied with leather thongs. To protect the head and neck,

The weaponry and armor of ancient Japanese samurai were as lethal as they were beautiful. This photo shows the bows, helmets, armor, swords, and daggers that were a standard part of dress in war. Bows and arrows were very popular as they could cause the death of an enemy without the victim being able to see his killer. During war, whistling arrows were shot to fend off evil spirits or to get the attention of certain gods.

they used iron helmets. These early forms of armor were decorative as well as extremely functional. Many helmets were made into beautiful objects with the use of decorative leather lacing or peacock feathers.

With the introduction of the horse during the fifth century AD, the emphasis moved from foot combat to archery and sword fighting on horseback. However, to handle a horse during a battle required additional

A Japanese woodcut illustrating a scene from a war story called "The Tale of Heikei" shows a warrior seated on a horse during battle. The warrior, Nasu no Yoichi, is attacking an enemy ship that is quickly making its approach to the Japanese shore.

innovations, including the introduction of stirrups, which originated in China. Constructed of wood, stirrups were flat and oval with a long handle. A metal covering, such as gilded bronze or iron plate, was placed over the wood. Sometimes, the stirrups were completely cast from bronze or iron.

To fight on horseback necessitated adjustments in armor. With their usual skill, the Japanese made armor more flexible by using iron and rawhide scales, called *sane*. First, the sane were lacquered before being tied. This process slowed decay. Later, silk replaced leather for the lacing. The armor also became more decorative, with geometric patterns or flowers incorporated into the designs. Helmets had detachable face guards, which were finely forged and lacquered. As such, they not only offered protection but also showcased the artisan's craftsmanship.

SPECIAL ARROWS—SPECIAL USES

The Japanese used different arrows to complete certain tasks. For instance, a narrow four-sided arrowhead such as the *yanagi*, or willow-leaf, and *sasa no ha*, or bamboo leaf was efficient at penetrating armor. A forked arrowhead, or *karimata*, could be used to cut rope or lacings. Some karimata were fitted with whistling devices, which were used to signal troops. Barbed broadhead arrows, or *hirane*, were mostly used for decoration or show. All these arrowheads were shaped like leaves. Although the blades were carefully made, in keeping with the skills that had been passed down from generations of Japanese craftsmen, many were rendered all the more beautiful with engraving. Some were even decorated with images or poetry.

Bows and Arrows

Bows were first developed between the third and sixth centuries BC. Initially made of unvarnished wood cut from boxwood and zelkova trees, bows were later fashioned from lacquered bamboo, which the Japanese found to be more flexible and durable. To build the bow, an artisan covered a wood core with a strip of bamboo and a laminate to provide additional strength. At first, glue made from lacquer was used, but it was then replaced by rattan. The bows were stored in tubular bags made of cloth, which were tied on either end. The average length of a bow was 6.5 feet (2 m).

Arrows, or *ya*, were made with a bamboo shaft that was carefully treated and straightened in a hot sand bed. The guide feathers were mostly from eagles, hawks, cranes, or pheasants. Arrowheads forged by special blacksmiths displayed intricate designs that demonstrated the Japanese aesthetic, superior in both quality and beauty.

This late thirteenth-century Japanese sword blade was crafted by a swordsmith named Masamune. The technical masters who create these lethal weapons sign their name on their wares by carving their signatures—known as *mei* in Japanese—into the tang *(nakago)* of the blade. The tang is the part of the blade that is inserted into the hilt or handle of the sword.

Even today, early Japanese weapons and armor are still considered among the finest in the world.

The *tsuru*, or bowstrings, were made of hemp or ramie, and were coated with wax. The upper end was tied to the bow with a red silk ribbon. The lower end was tied with a white one. The arrows were carried in a wood *ebira*, or quiver. These were constructed in a box shape with an open top.

Swordplay

Along with bows and arrows, the Japanese were famous for their swords. The first evidence of swords being used in Japan dates to the middle of the third century. These blades, called *chokuto*, were broad, straight, and single edged.

Straight swords were used until the eighth century. As warfare was conducted more frequently on horseback than on foot, new weaponry was developed. Demonstrating their talent for innovation and adaptation, the Japanese accommodated soldiers on horseback by designing single-edged and curved swords known as *tachi*. Another sword used in warfare was the *kogarasumaru*, a curved, two-edged sword.

THE TECHNOLOGY OF SCIENCE AND MEDICINE

During the sixth and seventh centuries AD, doctors, herb specialists, men who devised calendars, diviners, and mystics came to Japan. They brought with them the latest books on astronomy, calendar making, geography, and divination—all of which were used to train Japanese students.

Mathematics

Historians believe that after Buddhism was introduced to Japan from China in 552 AD, Chinese texts on arithmetic, algebra, and geometry spurred the evolution of Japanese mathematics. The earliest of these texts is thought to be the *Chou-pei Suan-ching*, which contains an example and proof of the Pythagorean theorem. This part of the text dates to at least the sixth century BC. Another important text from the third century BC is the *Chiu-chang*

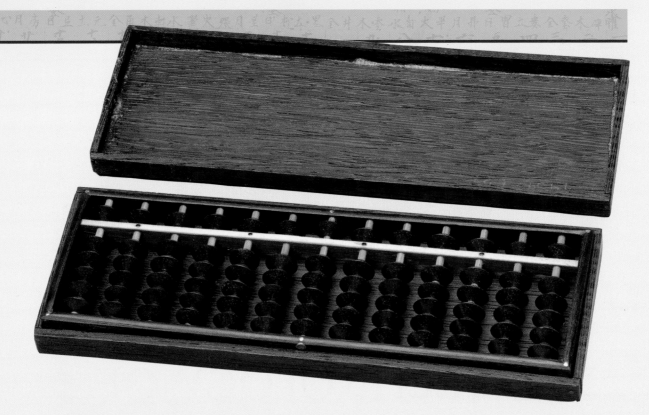

This is a photograph of a circa nineteenth-century Japanese abacus that was used for counting and solving mathematical equations. Called a *soroban* in Japanese, this is an example of an intermediary version between the original Chinese abacus and the modern Japanese counting tool. It has one bead above the bar and five below.

Suanshu. This text explained methods for finding the areas of triangles, circles, quadrilaterals, and other geometric shapes.

Ultimately, mathematics and geometry gave way to the study of astrology, making horoscopes, and the development of puzzles and games. It would be many more years before the Japanese began to make real headway in mathematics and geometry.

City Planning

The single exception was the use of mathematics and geometry in city planning. Again drawing on Chinese models, the Japanese designed their cities in a grid pattern, known as the Jô-Bô system. In the eighth century, Nara, the capital of Japan at the time, made use of this system. A central axis divided Nara into the Left City and the Right City. Each of these

Part of a classic example of ancient Japanese city planning is the Horyuji in Nara. This monastery complex, which was founded in 607, contains some of the oldest wooden buildings in the world. The detailed specificity with which Nara was designed allowed for easy identification. The grid system is very useful in planning cities, or areas within cities that are supremely easy to navigate.

sections was then subdivided into a matrix of nine *jô* (rows) and four *bô* (columns). A city block (also called a *bô*) was about 1,750 square feet (532 m) and was bordered by major thoroughfares. Each *bô* was again subdivided into four-by-four cells called *tsubo*, the size of which was 1,432 square feet (133 sq m). This system enabled the Japanese to identify every place in the city by specific row and column numbers.

Calendars and Clocks

One of the earliest types of Japanese calendars are the solar calendars known as the Kanayama megaliths. These stones are located in Kanayama, a mountainous area of central Japan. Believed to have been built during the mid-Joman period, these ancient stone structures are similar to the megaliths found at Stonehenge in Great Britain.

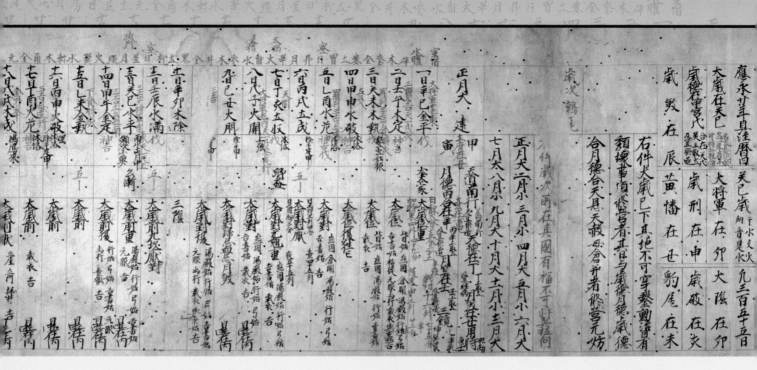

This type of calendar, called Guchureki, was used in ancient Japan until the Edo period. On the calendar, various words indicating seasons, annual events and holidays, and daily good omens were written in Chinese characters, or kanji. They were referred to as *rekichu*, which means "calendar notes." This type of calendar was mostly used by noblemen who often wrote personal notes in the blank spaces. These ancient "diaries" have given historians detailed insight into the life of the ancient Japanese.

A more formal calendar design was created in Japan from China via Korea. Historians believe that by AD 604, the Japanese had organized their first calendar, called Tai-in-taiyo-reki.

Tai-in-taiyo-reki was based on the solar and lunar cycles of the months. Because the moon orbits Earth in about 29.5 days, the Japanese had to adjust months to be either 29 or 30 days. They created Dai-no-tsuki (the long month) and Sho-no-tsuki (the short month). A solar year is defined by Earth's orbit around the sun in 365.25 days. Eventually, the Japanese realized that repeating the long and short months resulted in inconsistencies between the observed seasons and the calendar.

To compensate for this discrepancy, they created a month called Uru-zuki, which they inserted into their calendar

WHAT DAY IS IT?

Early Japanese calendars were broken down into six-day weeks. The six days—*taian, butsumetsu, senpu, tomobiki, shako,* and *sensho*—were associated with good and bad fortune. Taian, for example, was considered among the luckiest days. Butsumetsu was thought to be an unimportant day, while tomobiki was associated with bad luck.

every few years to create a year with thirteen months. They also changed the order of the longer and shorter months year by year. Establishing an accurate Japanese calendar was so important that it was placed under the supervision of the imperial court. The calendars were transcribed on long pieces of paper known as calendar rolls, which were then tucked into cylinders.

Medicine

In the early years of the ancient period, the Japanese, like many peoples, believed that the gods or evil spirits sent disease to punish or torment human beings. Treatment and prevention were mostly based on religious practices, such as prayers and incantations; later, drugs and bloodletting were also employed.

In 982, Tamba Yasuyori completed the thirty-volume *Ishinho*, the oldest Japanese medical text still in existence. This work discusses diseases and their treatment, classifying them mainly according to the affected organs or body parts. It is based on older Chinese medical books.

The Chinese also passed on their knowledge of such techniques as acupuncture and herbal medicine. The major difference between Chinese and Japanese herbal practice is that the Japanese drew on their familiarity with native plants and herbs to create their own medicines. One of the first developed was tea.

THE TECHNOLOGY OF TRANSPORTATION

Transportation can take many forms. Land travel requires a system of roads to accommodate foot traffic, animals, and vehicles. Traveling by sea presents a different set of challenges. In ancient Japan, transportation was not of great importance as people did not travel much. As such, for many centuries, the Japanese were without an organized transportation system.

Land Travel

The first travelers in Japan were the immigrants who crossed the Asian land bridge to the island on foot. Foot travel continued to be the preferred method for the majority of Japanese until the nineteenth century. In Japan, wheeled vehicles were not developed for many centuries due to the difficulties presented by Japanese geography. Covered by vast mountain ranges, surrounded by the sea,

This Japanese woodblock print shows a variety of ancient and modern methods of transport and transportation. Pictured at top is the first steam train in Japan. It made the journey from Shimbashi in Tokyo to Yokohama. Below that is a horse-drawn bus and a man wearing Western clothes and riding a bicycle. The bottom panel illustrates a variety of traditional hand-drawn carts and rickshaws. These were used to transport passengers as well as foods and supplies.

TRAVEL FOR THE ELITE

By the eleventh century, special carriages had been developed for members of Japan's royalty and nobility. The enclosed vehicles, based on a Chinese carriage design, stood high off the ground. Covered with rich coats of lacquer, the carriages were beautifully decorated with silk curtains and were identified by their green gabled roofs. Carriages owned by members of lesser nobility commonly had thatched roofs. People of lower status also traveled in carriages, but these were made from simple poles that held together a roof of stretched straw and a floor of wood boards. All carriages held as many as four passengers.

In ancient Japan, as a means for the government to control security, there were many rivers over which no bridges were built. This was to discourage enemies from gaining easy access to certain areas. As a result, it was impossible for some people to travel throughout Japan. However, nobles who had the money to afford it could hire people to carry them over the water or would pay to be carried in what were called litters—a type of shelter that was carried on the shoulders of four men.

and crisscrossed by rivers, Japan was inhospitable to wheeled vehicles.

Two-wheeled wagons and carts known as *kago* were the only kind of wheeled vehicles the Japanese used with regularity. They used horses as pack animals to carry goods along the highways and in mountainous regions. However, those who could afford to do so also kept horses in order to ride them.

A System of Roads

The oldest record describing road conditions in Japan appears in a Chinese history book compiled in the third century called *Gishi-wajin-den*. Early Japanese roads were little more than primitive trails.

However, the names of some of these roads, such as Kuga-no-michi, (Northland Road); Umitsu-michi (East Sea Road); and Higashi-no-yamamichi (East Mountain Road), were recorded in the *Nihon Shoki*, or the *Chronicles of Japan*, considered the oldest written Japanese record.

By the end of the seventh century AD, a more extensive system of roads linked the entire country and promoted commerce and travel.

Conclusion

The Japanese also built a number of way stations to provide services to traveling nobles and imperial officials. These were established at intervals of approximately 10 miles (16 km). About 400 such places existed. In the middle of the eighth century, the Japanese initiated a roadside tree system, planting fruit trees along the main roads to provide shade and refreshment to weary travelers.

The ancient Japanese may have borrowed much of their early technology, yet, no matter what or how much they borrowed, the Japanese always improved upon it, creating a technology that was even more specialized and unique than what they had taken. In so doing, the Japanese have left an amazing legacy at which we continue to marvel today.

TIMELINE

ca. 10,000 BC	First use of pottery on Japanese islands
ca. 7000 BC	First production of clay figures.
ca. 3000 BC	First Jomon communities; introduction of iron from Korea.
ca. 1000 BC	Start of rice cultivation by Yayoi.
ca. 250 BC	Iron manufacturing begins by Yayoi.
ca. 200 BC	First kofun mounds built in western Japan. First armor developed.
AD 283	Beginning of textile and sewing industry.
AD 276	Irrigation methods first used.
ca. AD 300	Keyhole-shaped burial mounds appear.
AD 350	First iron saws made.
AD 471	Forging of iron swords.
AD 500	Stirrups invented.
AD 552	Buddhism introduced to Japan.
AD 577	Construction of temples begins.
AD 604	Calendar is developed.
AD 610	Paper is first produced in Japan.

GLOSSARY

adze A cutting tool used chiefly for shaping wood.

algebra The mathematical study of quantities using letters and numbers.

artifact Any object created by human hands, especially from earlier history.

astrology The study of the positions of stars.

bloodletting A medical practice in which large quantities of blood were drained from a patient to cure or prevent illness.

brigands Robbers or a group of thieves.

forge To form metal by heating and hammering.

gild To cover with a thin layer of gold.

gimlet A small tool used for making holes.

guild An early association of merchants or craftsmen.

incantation The use of spells or magic.

laminate To roll into a thin plate or sheet of wood.

megalithic Using very large stones for a monument or as building blocks.

mystic A follower of a spiritual life.

pavilion A canopy or tent that is used for entertainment.

phonetics The study of the sounds of speech.

Pythagorean theorem A mathematical formula for calculating the longest length of a triangle.

quiver A case for holding and carrying arrows.

rawhide The hide of a cow or other animal before it is tanned.

thatch Straw, reeds, or other leaves used for roofing.

FOR MORE INFORMATION

Center for Japanese Studies
University of Hawaii at Manoa
1890 East-West Road, Moore 216
Honolulu, HI 96822 USA
Web site: http://www.hawaii.edu/cjs

History of Science and Technology
Smith College
Northampton, MA 01063
Web site: http://www.smith.edu/hsc

Japan Studies Program
East Asia Center
University of Washington
Thomson Hall 301
Box 353650
Seattle, WA 98195-3650
Web site: http://jsis.artsci.
washington.edu/programs/easc/
JapanStudiesProgram.html

Kyoto National Museum
527 Chayamachi, Higashimaya-ku
Kyoto, Japan 605-0931
Web site: http://www.kyohaku.go.jp/
eng/index_top.html

Tokyo National Museum
13-9 Ueno Park
Taitoku, Tokyo, Japan 11-8712
Web site: http://www.tnm.jp

Web Sites

Due to the changing nature of
Internet links, the Rosen Publishing
Group, Inc., has developed an online
list of Web sites. This site is updated
regularly. Please use this link to access
the list:

http://www.rosenlinks.com/taw/teaj

FOR FURTHER READING

Behnke, Alison. *Japan in Pictures*. Minneapolis, MN: Lerner Publications Company, 2003.

Grizner, Charles, Douglas A. Phillips, and Kristi Desaulniers. *Japan*. Philadelphia, PA: Chelsea House Publications, 2003.

Kiritani, Elizabeth. *Vanishing Japan: Traditions, Crafts and Culture*. New York, NY: Tuttle Publishing, 1995.

McNeil, Ian. *An Encyclopedia of the History of Technology*. New York, NY: Routledge, 1990.

Naff, Clay Farris. *Japan*. San Diego CA: Greenhaven Press, 2004.

Perkins, Dorothy. *Encyclopedia of Japan: Japanese History and Culture, From Abacus to Zori*. New York, NY: Facts on File, 1991.

Yenne, Bill. *100 Inventions That Shaped World History*. San Francisco, CA: Bluewood Books, 1993.

BIBLIOGRAPHY

Bito Masahide, and Watanabe Akio. *A Chronological Outline of Japanese History*. Tokyo, Japan: International Society for Educational Information.

Brown, Delmar M. *The Cambridge History of Japan*, Vol. 1. New York, NY: Cambridge University Press, 1993.

Hall, John Whitney. *Japan: From Prehistory to Modern Times*. New York, NY: Delta Books, 1973.

Hane, Mikiso. *Premodern Japan: A Historical Survey*. Boulder, CO: Westview Press, 1991.

Henshall, Kenneth. *A History of Japan: From Stone Age to Super Power*. New York, NY: St. Martin's Press, 1999.

James, Peter, and Nick Thorpe. *Ancient Inventions*. New York, NY: Ballantine Books, 1994.

Smith, David Eugene, and Yoshio Mikami. *A History of Japanese Mathematics*. New York, NY: Dover Publications, 2004.

Sinclaire, Clive. *Samurai: The Weapons and Spirit of the Japanese Warrior*. London, England: Lyons Press, 2001.

Uchida, Hoshimi. *Short History of the Japanese Technology*. Tokyo, Japan: The History of Technology Library, 1995. Retrieved November 10, 2004 (http://www.ied.co.jp/isan/sangyo-isan/JS7-history.htm).

INDEX

About the Author

Meg Greene is an award-winning writer and historian. She holds a B.S. in history from Lindenwood College, St. Charles, Missouri, and two master's degrees including an M.A. in history from the University of Nebraska at Omaha, and an M.S. in historic preservation from the University of Vermont. She is the author of more than thirty books, including *Slave Young, Slave Long: The American Slave Experience*, which was named a 1999 Honor Book in Social Studies by the Society of School Librarians International, and *Buttons, Bones, and the Organ-Grinder's Monkey: Tales of Historical Archaeology*, which was named a Best Book for Teens by the New York Public Library in 2001. Ms. Greene makes her home in Virginia.

Photo Credits

Editor: Annie Sommers;
Designer: Evelyn Horovicz;
Photo Researcher: Jeffrey Wendt